MW00892845

The Little Guitar

Story by

Eric Manos

Illustrations by

Eva Serencisova

DORRANCE PUBLISHING CO., INC.
PITTSBURGH, PENNSYLVANIA 15222

Illustrations by Eva Serencisova

Dorrance Publishing Co., Inc.
701 Smithfield Street
Pittsburgh, PA 15222
Visit our website at *www.dorrancebookstore.com*

ISBN: 978-1-4349-1229-9
eISBN: 978-1-4349-3941-8

For little Eva

Once upon a time, a little guitar was born. She was handmade in a small workshop by the loving hands of a skilled craftsman. Her body was small, beautifully shaped and made of the finest woods.

The little guitar loved to be played, nestled in the gentle arms of a gifted musician. And when her strings were expertly strummed or plucked, she sang out in clear ringing tones like those of angels singing.

On occasion, music students would visit the craftsman's shop. The little guitar also loved to be played by these students and she did her best to help them fill the air with beautiful music.

For the little guitar, there was no greater joy than to share the gift of her musical voice with the people around her. Seeing the smiles on their faces as she sang made her feel alive and loved.

One day the little guitar left the craftsman's shop. A man searching for a quality instrument bought the little guitar as a present for his son, a teenaged boy who wanted to learn to play.

The little guitar left the shop full of hope and excitement, looking forward to her new home, where she could sing and bring music and joy to new family and friends.

Things started off well in the little guitar's new home. The boy took her with him to his music lessons and practiced with her at home in an effort to learn how to play.

The little guitar wanted with all her heart to help and encourage the boy. She lovingly tried to make it easy for the boy to press down her strings, and she sang in pure melodic tones even when wrong notes were played.

After a few months of practice however, the boy became frustrated. Learning to play the little guitar was not fast and easy. In spite of the little guitar's efforts to sing sweetly, the boy soon lost interest.

The little guitar was shoved in the corner of a closet in the boy's room. Her strings were no longer allowed to ring out, her beautiful clear voice was no longer allowed to sing.

The little guitar was ignored most of the time, except when she was bumped. Her beautifully crafted body began to gather dust, and her flawless finish became bruised, scratched and stained.

Several of her strings broke and she began to lose her melodic voice. The little guitar began to worry that she would never sing again, that never again would she bring music and joy into people's lives.

One day the little guitar was placed in a wooden case and stowed away in the attic of the boy's house. Alone and forgotten, the little guitar thought her young life was over.

Several years later, the little guitar felt her wooden case being moved and after having spent most of her life in darkness, the case was opened and the little guitar felt light and warm sunshine on her body.

Her owner was moving house and was selling old and discarded things that would no longer be needed in the new home. The little guitar was placed on the front lawn among other items, waiting to be sold.

Many people visited the lawn sale and several items were indeed sold. Each time someone would look at the little guitar however, they would only shake their heads sadly and walk away.

FOR SALE!
ELVIS

For you see, during the time the little guitar was left in the attic, the changes from summer heat to winter cold caused her glue joints to weaken, to where now she was little more than so many loose pieces of wood in a box.

Her voice gone and her spirit broken, her once beautiful body was now broken as well. No longer needed or able to bring music into people's lives, the little guitar would have cried if guitars had tears to be able to cry.

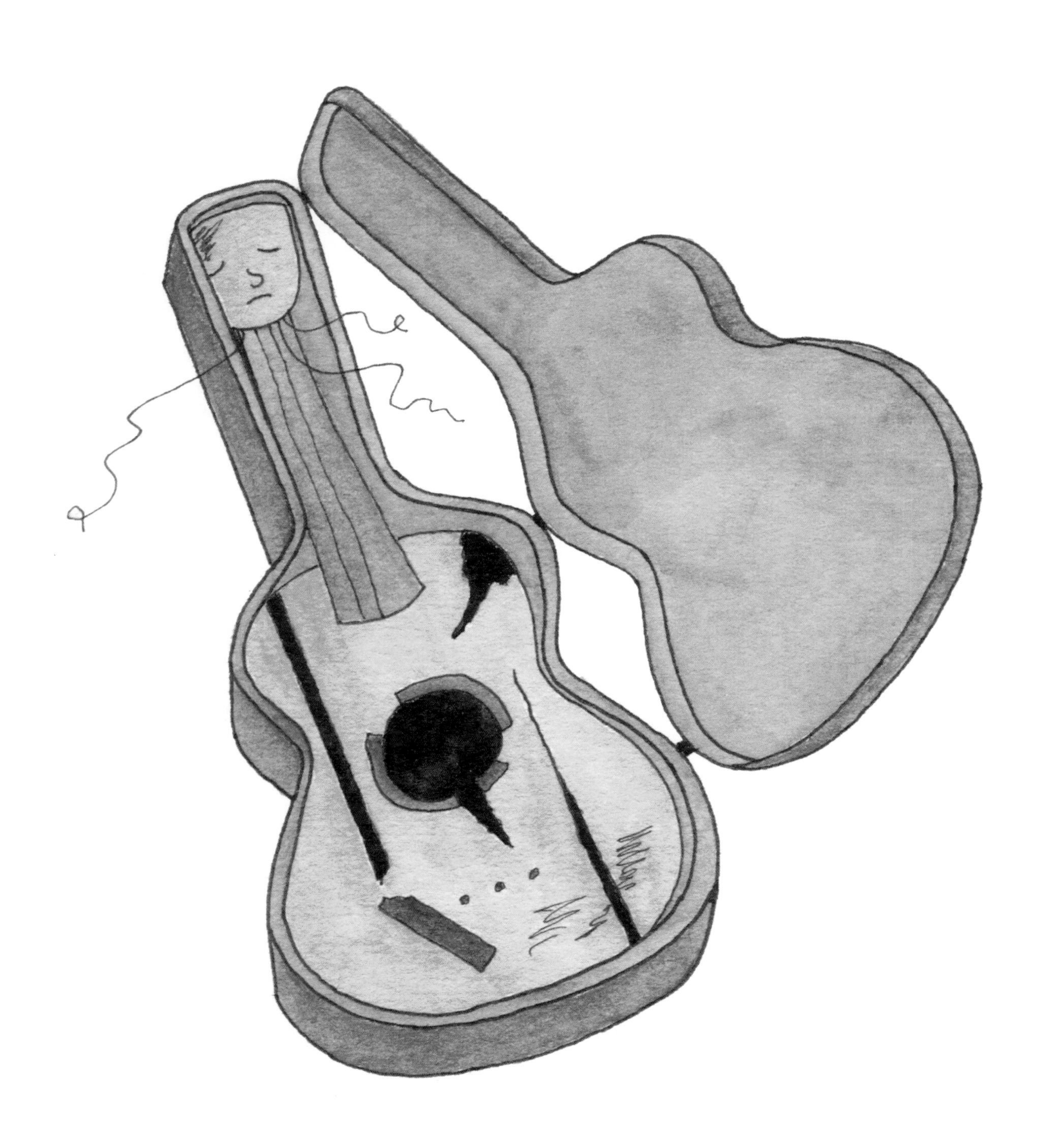

As the day drew to a close, the little guitar in her wooden case was the last item left on the front lawn. She prepared herself to be broken up and to end her life as firewood.

Moments before her wooden case would be shut forevermore, an old man walked by and saw the little guitar lying broken in her case. He slowly came over and asked if he could take a closer look.

The old man's hands were knotted and scarred but strong and gentle. He carefully lifted the little guitar from her case and saw that although she was bruised and broken, her wood was still fit and supple.

The old man lived alone in a small house that he had built by himself. As a young man, woodworking and playing guitar were what he loved most in the world. As he grew older however, he found it harder to work with his hands.

By and by he no longer spent his time working the wood he so loved, nor was he able to continue making sweet music with a guitar. The man became lonely and began to feel lost and forgotten.

After a closer look at the little guitar, the old man asked if he could buy it and was told that he could have it for nothing, as it was no longer worth selling. At that, the old man placed the little guitar back in her case and gently carried her home.

Back at home, the old man brought the little guitar to his workshop. He wished with all his heart that he could help the little guitar to sing again. As he looked at his tools, he suddenly felt in his heart that he COULD help!

He gently lifted the little guitar from her case and set her on his workbench. As he slowly began to examine the pieces of wood, his hands grew steady and his fingers started to work again as they had when he was a younger man.

TOOLS

Over the next several weeks, the old man worked most days and nights to bring the little guitar back to life and help her to sing again. As he did so, he too felt more and more as if HE was coming back to life.

Finally one day, the little guitar was ready for a new set of strings. The old man had done his job well, and the skills he had learned as a young man clearly showed through in the newly reborn little guitar.

Her small body was beautifully shaped again. The fine woods from which she was made were healed of their bruises, and her glossy finish reflected light like the surface of a clear, calm lake.

But beauty on the outside does not always mean beauty within. Were the old man's skills able to bring back the musical voice that once was? Could the little guitar sing again as in the past, like the voices of angels?

The old man carefully mounted fresh new strings on the little guitar and nervously tuned each string to its perfect pitch. With trembling hands, the old man gently nestled the little guitar in his arms.

The first strummed chord filled the room with heavenly sounds, bringing a blissful smile to the old man's face and tears of joy to his eyes. The little guitar sang effortlessly, free at last to again create beautiful music.

As the little guitar sang, the old man's stiff fingers began to relax. As he felt and heard the lilting angelic tones, his fingers became more alive, and the music that was locked in his soul started to be released.

The little guitar and the old man created hours of wondrous music together. And as they did so, the loneliness and sorrow of the years past fell away and disappeared like drops of rain on a warm summer's day.

If you listen closely, you can still hear them playing beautiful music together. The little guitar and the old man—two souls bound together forever, the gentle soul of the old man and the healing soul dwelling within the little guitar.

The End